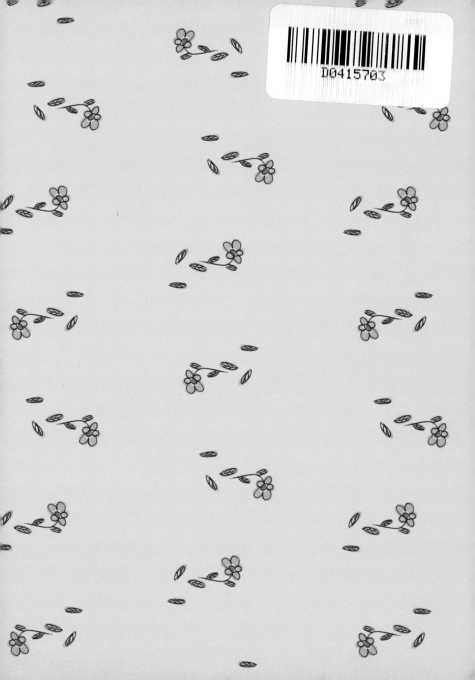

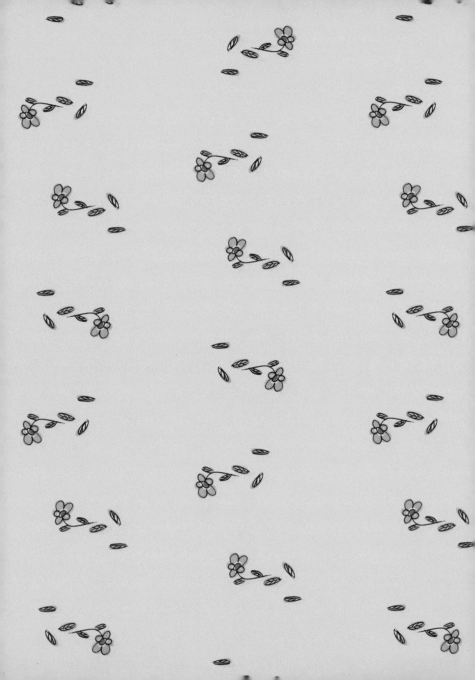

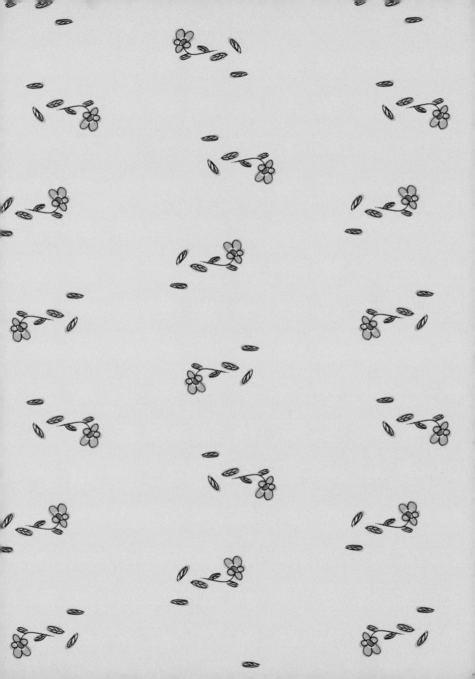

First published in the USA by Alfred A. Knopf, an imprint of
Random House Children's Books, a division of Random House LLC,
a Penguin Random House Company, in 2014
First published in this edition in the UK in 2017
by Faber & Faber Limited
Bloomsbury House,
74–77 Great Russell Street,
London WC1B 3DA

A CIP record for this book is available from the British Library

Printed in Malta

ISBN 978–0571–32973–1

4 6 8 10 9 7 5 3

To Magali Messac, the ballerina
on the cover of the magazine

Ballerina

Dreams

Ballerina Dreams

A true story

By Michaela DePrince and Elaine DePrince
Pictures by Ella Okstad

ff

FABER & FABER

Contents

1

The Ballerina

It is a chilly night in December. I stand backstage wearing leg warmers and a sweatshirt, but I'm still shivering.

"Five minutes, Michaela!" I hear. It's time for me to dance. I stretch my

legs and point my toes to get them ready.

I check my tiara to make sure it's not loose, and fluff out my pink tutu.

The knots in my pointe shoe ribbons are tied nice and tight. I wouldn't want them to slip off during the performance.

I peek through the stage curtains and see the eager faces of the audience.

They are waiting for the ballerina to appear.

The music begins, and my heart beats fast with excitement. I fly on to the stage. I am the ballerina!

The Orphan Girl

Long before I became a ballerina, I was

an orphan in Sierra Leone, a country

in western Africa. My parents died

there in the ongoing war. I was sent to

an orphanage, where children without

parents live.

There were twenty-seven children in the orphanage, but I was the only one with a condition called vitiligo. The vitiligo made some of my skin lose its colour. I have white spots on my brown skin.

Some of the other children laughed at my spots. They called me names, and I often felt sad.

One girl never laughed at me. Her
name was Mia, and she became my best
friend. We shared a grass mat to sleep

on at bedtime. We shared our rice at mealtimes. Mia sang to me and told me stories. I taught Mia how to play new games.

Sometimes I would miss my parents very much, but I would not cry in front of the other children. Instead, I would sit at the orphanage gate alone and let my tears flow.

One windy day, a magazine blew

down the road in front of the gate. I

reached out and caught it.

A pretty picture of a woman was

on the front cover of the magazine. She

wore a short pink dress that stuck out

around her in a circle. She had pink
shoes on her feet and stood on the tips of
her toes. She looked very happy.

"I want to be happy and beautiful
like you someday!" I said to the woman
in the picture as I wiped away my tears.

I showed the picture to Mia and
then folded it and hid it in my clothes. I
didn't want anybody to take it away
from me.

The next day, I showed my teacher the picture.

"Who is this woman? What is she doing? Why is she wearing these strange pink clothes?" I asked Teacher Sarah.

"This woman is a famous ballerina. She is wearing a tutu and pointe shoes because she is dancing ballet," Teacher Sarah explained.

"Do you think I can be a ballerina

like her someday?" I asked.

"You can become a ballerina, too, if you take lessons for many years, if you work hard, and if you practise every day."

Whoa! So many ifs! "If I can take lessons, I will work hard. I will practise every day!" I exclaimed. "I want to become a ballerina."

3

Getting Adopted

One night, Papa Andrew, the director

of the orphanage, told all of us, "It is

time to leave Sierra Leone. We must

go to a country where there is no war.

There you will meet the families

who will adopt you."

We travelled on foot with Papa Andrew, walking over the mountains and through the jungle. At night, the sounds of the jungle terrified us. We slept close together, trembling with fear. Mia sang to me to help me feel better, and I played hand-clapping games with her.

Finally we reached safety, and

Papa Andrew took us to meet our new mothers and fathers.

I held Mia's hand. My knees began to shake and my heart began to pound. What if I never saw Mia again? I worried that my new parents wouldn't like my spots. I worried that they would not let me dance ballet.

A woman with hair the colour of daisies opened her arms and hugged

Mia. I was happy that Mia had a new
mother but felt sad that we wouldn't live
together any more. But then the lady
pulled me into her arms, too!

Mia and I were going to live together. This woman was our new mama. My best friend and I would be sisters! Then I did cry. I cried tears of joy.

Our new mama had a lot of presents for my sister and me. Mia loved the trainers with lights on the bottom. I searched through my mother's bags, but I could not find pink shoes for dancing ballet.

My mother wanted to know what I was looking for. I could not remember the English words that Teacher Sarah had taught me. Instead, I showed my mother the picture of the ballerina and I danced around on my toes.

My mama understood. She knelt down and said to me, "When we get home, you will dance ballet."

4

My New Life

My new home was in America. We had food, warm clothes and lots of love. Mia and I went to many fun places with our parents and our new brothers.

One day, Mama took us to a shop.

There I found a video with ballerinas on the box. "Mama!" I called out with excitement. "I found a ballet film!"

The film was *The Nutcracker*, performed by the New York City Ballet.

Mama bought it.

That night, Mia and I watched the video until we fell asleep. The next morning, we woke up and watched it again. We tried to copy the dancers.

I loved to pretend I was the Sugar Plum

Fairy. I dreamed of the day I would

dance onstage in the real *Nutcracker*.

Soon I would know enough English

to take ballet lessons!

5

Ballet Lessons

"Wake up, Michaela! Wake up, Mia!

Today is the day of your first ballet

lesson," Mama called one Saturday

morning.

My eyes popped open and I leaped

out of bed.

In ballet class, our teacher explained to the students that all ballet words are French. She said, "That is because the first professional ballet company, the Paris Opera Ballet, was started in France, more than three hundred and fifty years ago."

At the beginning of every class, we lined up and held the barre.

Next, we learned how to stand in
the five positions of ballet. Then we
practised how to hold our arms.
"This is called
port de bras,
which means
'position of
the arms',"
our teacher
explained.

The teacher
showed us how to
tendu, which means
"stretched" in French.
I watched her carefully.

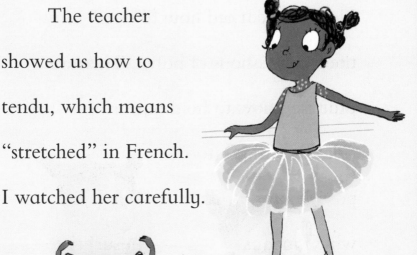

When she stood
in fifth position,
I did too.

"Stretch out your leg and point your toes," she said as we put out our right legs. Next, she stepped on to her right foot. I did, too.

I looked down in surprise. I had tendued from fifth position to second position!

Now our teacher said, "Bend your
knees a little. And straighten them again.
Good. You just did
a plié."
I learned that plié
means "bent" in
French.

Putting ballet
steps together is
called a combination. That day, I did

35

my first ballet combination! I felt
so proud!

During one class, my ballet teacher
put her sweatshirt in the middle of the
floor. Then she leaped over it. "That is
a grand jeté," she said. "Now you will
try it."

When I leaped across the floor, I
felt like I was flying. I loved that feeling.
The grand jeté became my favourite step.

I learned more steps with each

lesson. I did a leap that made me look

like a cat with hot feet. I laughed when I

learned that it was called a pas de chat,

or "cat step".

Every day, I practised new steps and combinations. When I was seven and a half years old, my teacher decided that I was ready to dance on my toes. This is called dancing en pointe.

I needed to buy special shoes to dance en pointe. My new pointe shoes were silky soft and beautiful. When I put them on my feet, I looked like the ballerina on the cover of the magazine.

Now I practised harder than before.

Soon I was dancing en pointe on the

stage.

6

My First *Nutcracker*

When I was eight years old, I auditioned

for *The Nutcracker.*

I looked for black children in the

party scene of the video that I owned,

but I didn't see any. I worried that I

would not get chosen for *The Nutcracker.*

When I went to audition, I danced

my very best. I hoped that I would be

cast as a party girl or a polichinelle, one of the little children who dance out from under Mother Ginger's dress.

At the end of the audition, *The Nutcracker* director gave each of us an envelope. "Do not open this until you get downstairs!" he warned. My knees shook all the way down the steps. Finally I reached the first floor and opened the envelope. When I saw the words "party girl" and "polichinelle girl", I thought I

would faint!

That year, I had a thrilling time dancing in *The Nutcracker*. Best of all, I decided that if I could be a black party girl and a black polichinelle girl, then someday I could surely be a black Sugar Plum Fairy.

7

In Front of a Camera

One day, I got a phone call from a film producer named Bess Kargman, who wanted to make a film about ballet. "It's a documentary," Bess explained. "I would like you to be in it, Michaela."

I was shy, so at first I said, "No, thank you."

Mama said, "Bess's film will give you a chance to show the world that black girls can be ballerinas."

There are few professional black ballerinas. Many people have never seen a black ballerina. So I thought about what Mama said. Then I changed my mind.

"Yes," I told Bess. "I would like to be in your film."

Bess and her film crew followed me around with cameras. They filmed me

practising ballet and dancing in a big competition in New York City called the Youth America Grand Prix.

During the competition, I injured my left ankle. It felt hot and swollen, and I wasn't sure I would be able to dance.

I decided to continue anyway and ended up winning a scholarship to the famous Jacqueline Kennedy Onassis School of American Ballet Theatre in

New York City.

People all over the world saw Bess's film, which is called *First Position*. And it won many important awards.

Some people who saw the film wanted to know more about me. They invited me to be on television programmes and featured me in magazines. They asked me questions about being a black ballerina.

49

I was still shy, so sometimes it was hard for me to answer questions. Then I would remember the many messages that children everywhere sent me after they saw *First Position*.

One girl wrote, "You are my hero." Another wrote, "I want to grow up to dance like you." Messages like these made me feel brave. Maybe I could inspire other children to study ballet, just

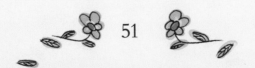

as the woman in the magazine picture

had inspired me.

8

A Dream Come True

My dream has come true. I am now a real ballerina, a professional dancer. That means I dance for a living. My favourite step is still the grand jeté. Many people call me the ballerina who flies.

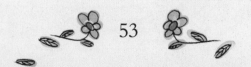

I have been lucky to dance wonderful roles in many different ballets. I have even danced the role of the Sugar Plum Fairy in *The Nutcracker*.

My dancing has taken me to many countries. Sometimes I dance on grand stages; other times I dance in small auditoriums. Once I even performed in a barn. I have danced for rich people and poor people, for all ages and races.

Dancing brings me great joy. I love knowing that my dancing also brings joy to others.

I have learned not to be shy. When I travel, I enjoy talking to people, especially children. Many kids ask me, "How can I make my dream come true?"

I tell them, "It doesn't matter if you dream of being a doctor, a teacher, a writer, or a ballerina. Every dream

begins with one step. After that, you

must work hard and practise every day.

If you never give up, your dream will

come true."

About the Authors

Michaela DePrince studied on scholarship at the Rock School of Dance Education and the Jacqueline Kennedy Onassis School at the American Ballet Theatre. Michaela is now a professional ballerina. She was named the youngest principal dancer for the Dance Theatre of Harlem and is dancing with the Dutch National Ballet, one of the top classical ballet companies in the world.

Michaela starred in the ballet documentary *First Position*, which was nominated for an NAACP Image Award. She has also appeared on *Dancing with the Stars*, as well as *Good Morning America*, *Nightline*, BBC News and other news programmes in the United States and internationally. In 2014, *The Times* named Michaela one of their 'Top 25 Under 20' and *Elle UK* named her one of their '30 Under 30'. You can visit her online at michaeladeprince.com or on Twitter at @michdeprince.

Elaine DePrince is Michaela's adoptive mother and co-author. She is the author of *Cry Bloody Murder: A Tale of Tainted Blood*, as well as a songwriter, and owner of Sweet Mocha Music LLC, an Indie record label and music publishing business. A graduate of Rutgers University and a former special education teacher, Elaine, after raising five sons, took a leave of absence from law school in 1999 to adopt a child from war-torn West Africa. She often says that the need was so great that she ended up with six West African daughters.

Elaine lives near Atlanta, Georgia, with her husband and four of their daughters.

About the Illustrator

Ella Okstad has been working as an illustrator since graduating from Kent Institute of Art and Design in 2000. After 4 years in the UK, she moved back to her native country, Norway where she now works from her home based studio in Trondheim. Ella works on various children's book projects, including the *Squishy McFluff* series.

Ella lives with her husband, three boys and a cat.

Growing up with
FABER

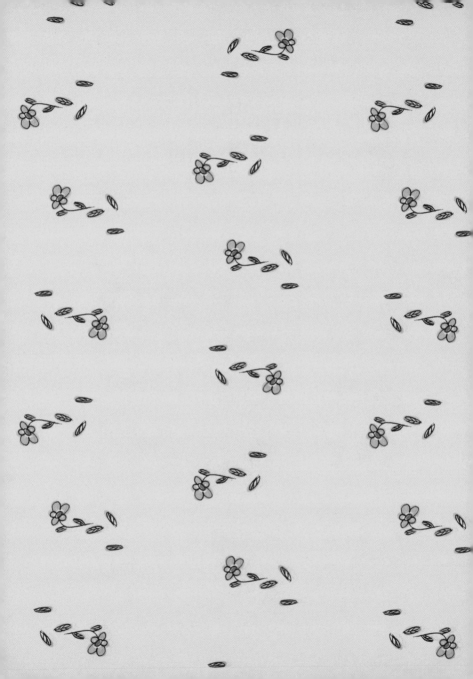

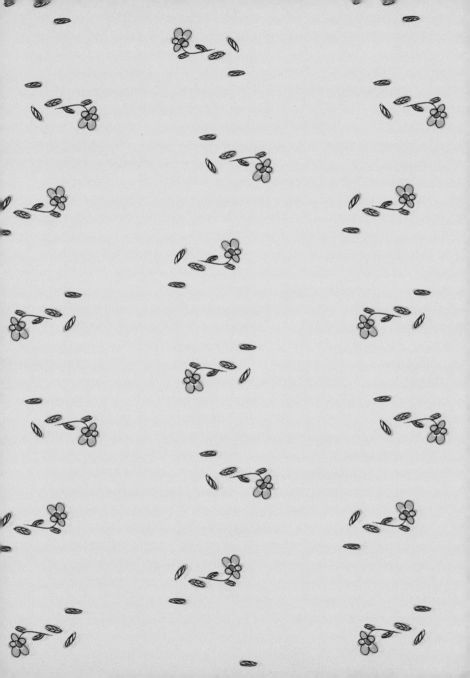

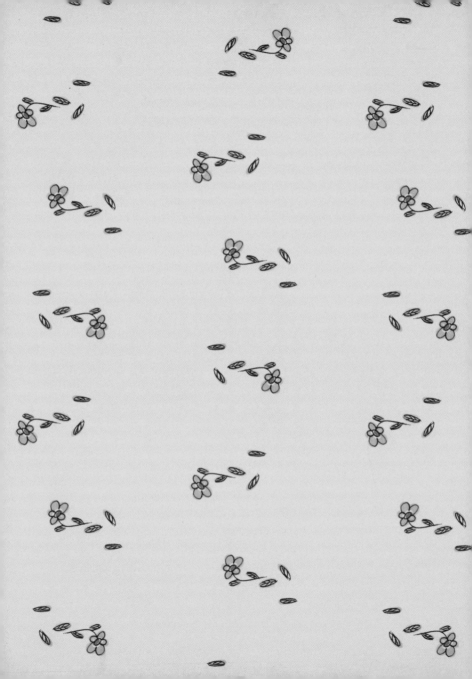